THE BOOK OF
TIME OUTS

A Mostly True History of the World's Biggest Troublemakers

Written and illustrated by
DEB LUCKE

SIMON & SCHUSTER BOOKS FOR YOUNG READERS New York · London · Toronto · Sydney

SIMON & SCHUSTER BOOKS FOR YOUNG READERS · An
imprint of Simon & Schuster Children's Publishing Division
· 1230 Avenue of the Americas, New York, New York
10020 · Copyright © 2008 by Deb Lucke · All rights reserved,
including the right of reproduction in whole or in part in any
form. · SIMON & SCHUSTER BOOKS FOR YOUNG READERS is a trademark of
Simon & Schuster, Inc. · Book design by Jessica Sonkin · The text
for this book is set in Alghera Bold. · The illustrations for this book
are rendered in gouache. · Manufactured in China · 10 9 8 7 6 5 4 3 2 ·
Library of Congress Cataloging-in-Publication Data · Lucke, Deb. · The book
of time outs / written and illustrated by Deb Lucke. · p. cm. · "Spring 2008." ·
ISBN-13: 978-1-4169-2829-4 · ISBN-10: 1-4169-2829-4 · 1. Celebrities—Anecdotes—
Juvenile literature. 2. Time-out method—Anecdotes—Juvenile literature. I. Title. ·
CT107.L83 2007 · 920.02—dc22 · 2006013408

For as long as there have been people,

there have been people who were badly behaved, out of line, out of order, ill-mannered, inappropriate, or just plain unwilling to follow the rules. Since you're reading this book perhaps you too have, on occasion, been less than perfect.

Maybe you woke up feeling full of yourself and like doing whatever you wanted. You got more and more out of control. Finally someone like your mom noticed and said, "You need a time out!"

And suddenly, surprise!— you were on a little vacation from everyone else. In a corner, by yourself, where you could pout away until you could play nicely with others.

If so, you're not the first to have a time out, you're not the worst.

· HANNIBAL THE ANIMAL ·

Several thousand years ago the Carthaginians set out to crush Rome. Since tanks hadn't been invented yet, their general, Hannibal, used the next best thing. Elephants!

The Romans were so terrified of these big gray weapons of mass destruction that Hannibal won every single battle. He started describing himself as "the greatest general that ever lived."

That is, until the Romans turned around and attacked Carthage. This time, nothing in that battle went according to the battle plan. When the trumpets sounded "charge!" the elephants panicked, then trampled off in completely the wrong direction. Hannibal yelled, "Stampede!" But it was too late. His army was flattened.

Then "the greatest general that ever lived" had a very long time out in a far-off corner of the ancient world.

· THE PHIGHTING PHARAOH ·

Back when the pyramids weren't all that old, Cleopatra and her brother, Ptolemy, shared the throne of Egypt. Like a lot of sisters and brothers, they weren't very good at sharing. They squabbled until all of Egypt was ready to scream.

Then one day the royal guardians came in to find Cleopatra sitting on the throne alone, ruling the country all by herself. Ptolemy was sitting on the floor crying. Before Cleopatra could say, "Hey, he started it!" the royal guardians had carted her off to the middle of the desert for a time out.

But that didn't stop Cleopatra. She made friends with a Roman named Julius Caesar who just happened to have an army. Caesar toppled Ptolemy off the throne and Cleopatra sat right back down.

AND FURTHERMORE...

· MARCUS TULLIUS "PUT-A-SOCK-IN-IT" CICERO ·

Back in 58 BCE Cicero was so good at giving speeches, the Romans called him the "Golden Tongue." He could change men's minds with just a few words. But he rarely used just a few.

He could talk for days about duty. And weeks about law. No one else could get a word in edgewise. He had the first word, the middle word, and the last word in every argument.

Finally just about everyone grew tired of the sound of his voice. Especially the people he was arguing with. So they gave him a time out 500 miles from Rome.

Still, Cicero managed to get in the last word. He sent back long letters from his time out that were so eloquent that they ended up in the library. You can still read them today.

· LIONHEARTED, BUT KNUCKLEHEADED ·

Richard the Lionheart was a knight in the age of chivalry, which meant he was brave in battle, but also very polite. Then one day he forgot his manners entirely.

On his way home from the Crusades, he and some friends took a shortcut through Leopold V of Austria's yard. Leopold was very sensitive about English feet trodding on his Austrian grass. He came running out of his castle and yelled something like, "You boys get off of my lawn!"

Richard and his friends were given a time out in a castle dungeon for trespassing until his mother could send an enormous amount of money to bail him out. It was all very embarrassing.

· THE NOT-SO-CLEAN QUEEN ·

Isabella of Castile bragged that she only bathed twice in her whole life. Once was when she was baptized. The second time was on her wedding day.

Perhaps that's why her older half brother, the king, gave her a time out in Segovia while he and the court stayed in Madrid. Historians say it was politics, but a far better explanation is that he was removing her from smelling range.

He was firming up plans to marry her off to a foreign prince and send her to a faraway land when she snuck out and married Ferdinand of Aragon. The king was mad as heck at what he saw as an act of rebellion, although he didn't condemn her since it meant that after 18 years she'd finally had a bath!

· THE EXPLORER THAT WENT TOO FAR ·

In 1492 Columbus set off to discover a new route to India. Instead, he found a bunch of islands with not much on them, but still he thought he could make something of it.

Back in Spain for "show-and-tell," he presented Queen Isabella* with a sweet potato. She wasn't impressed. He handed her a turkey. She frowned and drummed her fingernails impatiently on the edge of her throne. Columbus began to sweat. "Why, the place is just littered with gold and gems!" he said with his fingers crossed behind his back.

A boatload of excited Spaniards sailed back with Columbus to get rich. But when they found out he'd told them a whopper, they were outraged and rebelled.

Then Columbus discovered what happens when you don't tell the truth. He got a time out with leg irons and a trip back to Spain to explain it all to the queen.

*The very same Isabella who wouldn't wash. Most likely, Columbus held his breath while he knelt before her.

· GRANDMA, THE PIRATE ·

Grace O'Malley was a little old lady who spent a lot of time lurking behind Irish islands waiting for English ships to sail by. That's because she was a ferocious pirate. She'd snag the ships with her grappling hook, leap aboard, and rob them blind.

Twice the English navy caught her in the act and gave her a time out. But as soon as she got out of ye olde gaol, she'd go right back to plundering and the top of Her Majesty's most wanted list.

After 60 years of ceaseless marauding, Grace tired of the game. She sailed over to England to ask Her Majesty herself, Queen Elizabeth I, for a pardon.

"Alrighty then," said the queen, "as long as you promise not to do it again."

· ACH! THAT BACH! ·

Johann Sebastian Bach was one of the greatest composers of all time, yet even he couldn't coax a good performance from the musicians at the Church of St. Boniface.

Time after time, the bassoonist kept playing it wrong. Finally Bach lost his temper. Instead of saying, "I believe you're a little flat," he called the man a "nanny-goat bassoonist."

Later on, the "nanny-goat bassoonist" got even by hitting the composer with a stick and calling him a "dirty dog." The authorities showed up and the two of them were separated. Bach was reprimanded for the insult and a report went into his record.

Over the years, more and more reports were added. In 1717 Bach was given a time out for "stubbornness"! The man simply could not live in harmony.

· THE ARMÉE BRAT ·

Napoleon Bonaparte was a Frenchman who took things that didn't belong to him. Like other people's countries. He looked at Germany and said, "Mine."

He saw Italy and said, "Mine." He pointed to Holland, Spain, Austria, Russia, and England and said, "Mine, all mine."

Needless to say, the people of Germany, Italy, Holland, Spain, Austria, Russia, and England didn't agree. This led to many battles over what was whose. Unfortunately, Napoleon kept winning the battles.

Finally in 1814 he lost one. He was given a time out on an island so tiny that no one cared if he thought it was "his."

That should have been the end of the story, but Napoleon said he had to go to the bathroom. Instead of returning to his time out, he snuck off to the Battle of Waterloo. Then he had an even longer time out on a different, harder-to-escape-from island.

· NOT THE SMARTEST ARTIST ·

Honoré Daumier was an artist who never flattered his subjects. In fact, he made fun of them. Let's say he was drawing a picture of a person whose ears stuck out. Daumier would make that person look like a monkey. If someone had a long nose, he'd make it so long it would look like something a bird could perch on.

One winter's day in 1832 he drew a picture of Louis Philippe, the king of France, who was rather bottom heavy. Daumier made him look like a pear. Everyone gathered around and laughed, except for the king. He didn't even smile.

He simply said, "You need a time out."

And just like that, Daumier was in a cell at Saint-Pélagie without even a pencil to keep him company.

· THE INSUFFERABLE SUFFRAGETTE ·

Susan B. Anthony did not know the meaning of the word "NO." She tried to vote even though women were NOT allowed to, and the men who ran the voting booth told her "NOT TO GO IN THERE." When she went in anyway, she NOT only got a time out; she also got a fine.

Later on, she admitted she deliberately broke the rule to show how stupid it was.

A lot of Americans agreed (especially the female Americans).

In 1920 the law was changed so women could vote.

· BAD, BAD, BABE ·

Babe Ruth hit a total of 714 home runs in his baseball career. Sometimes he'd hit 4 in 1 game! He also ate 27 hot dogs in 1 sitting, stayed out until 6 in the morning, was kicked out of the game 5 times for arguing with umpires in 1 season, and belched without saying, "Excuse me" too many times to count.

Babe's behavior was so bad that the Yankees' manager, Miller Huggins, sometimes felt more like a babysitter. It was reported that on a train to a game, Babe hung him out the window while the train was going at full speed!

Finally Miller decided it was time for Babe to grow up. The next time Babe goofed up, he got a fine of $5,000 and a 9-day-long time out from baseball (which is what really hurt). He was only allowed to play again after he apologized to Miller in front of the entire team.

Home for Wayward Boys
Sweet
Home for Wayward Boys

· THE HORN PLAYER THAT NEARLY BLEW IT ·

Once upon a time Louis Armstrong was just a poor boy looking for trouble. It found him, on New Year's Eve in 1912 in the city of New Orleans. A short while after that, the police showed up.

He was hauled away in a paddy wagon and put in a "home" for wayward children. Louis thought it was the end of the world. But it turned out it wasn't. His time out changed everything. While he was there he learned how to play the cornet.

When his time out was over, he played anywhere people would listen. He "blew up a storm" at church picnics, in honky-tonks, on riverboats. The people didn't just listen, they snapped their fingers, stomped their feet and hooted for joy.

He kept on tootin' away until millions of people were clap, clap, clapping all over the world.

· A VERY UPSTANDING SITTER ·

On December 1, 1955, Rosa Parks was sitting on a crowded bus when a man told her he wanted her seat. This was the law because he was white and she wasn't. But Rosa refused to budge. The police were called and she was given a time out.

During her time out, Rosa sat and thought and sat and thought and still she couldn't see what *she'd* done wrong. Therefore, she reasoned, *the law* must be wrong. So when her time out was over, she went out and campaigned to get the unfair law changed.

Rosa won the Congressional Medal of Honor for her efforts to make the world a fairer place.

Checklist

☐ LYING

☐ STEALING

☐ HITTING

☐ NAME-CALLING

☐ BITING

☒ NONE OF
   THE ABOVE

Every single one of these people

found out that actions have consequences.

Some got really out of control before they were given a time out. It was kind of scary.

Some learned from their time outs, some didn't. The ones that didn't ended up spending a lot of time *alone*.

Almost everyone thought they didn't deserve a time out. A few were right.

It's possible that one or two of our time-outers looked deep into their hearts and thought, "Maybe, just maybe, I *did* need to cool down a bit." We can't know for sure.

The one thing we can know for sure is that someday, somewhere, someone will once again be badly behaved, out of line, out of order, ill-mannered, inappropriate, or just plain unwilling to follow the rules. And they'll need a time out.

Let's just hope that someone isn't you or me.

Thanks to Paul Hartzell for his help with the wittier bits.